SNOW HAPPY!

by Patricia Hubbell * illustrated by Hiroe Nakata

TRICYCLE PRESS
Berkeley

Again, for Hal –P.H.

For Koharu –H.N.

All rights reserved. Published in the United States by Tricycle Press, an imprint of
Random House Children's Books, a division of Random House, Inc., New York.
www.randomhouse.com/kids

Tricycle Press and the Tricycle Press colophon are registered trademarks of Random House, Inc.

Library of Congress Cataloging-in-Publication Data
Hubbell, Patricia.
Snow happy / by Patricia Hubbell ; illustrations by Hiroe Nakata.–1st ed.
p. cm.
Summary: Children delight in playing in the snow, building an igloo, sliding, gliding, and getting wet and tired.
[1. Stories in rhyme. 2. Snow–Fiction.] I. Nakata, Hiroe, ill. II. Title.
PZ8.3.H848Sn 2011
[E]–dc22

ISBN 978-1-58246-329-2 (hardcover)
ISBN 978-1-58246-363-6 (Gibraltar lib. bdg.)

Printed in China

Design by Katie Jennings

Typeset in Aged

The illustrations in this book were rendered in ink, watercolor, and gouache.

1 2 3 4 5 6 - 14 13 12 11 10

First Edition

We're silly-willy laughy,
feeling slightly daffy,
leaping through the snow—

Snow
Happy!

We're skiing and we're sliding.
Down our hill we're gliding.
We trudge back up and shout—

Snow
Happy!

Dogs are yippy-yapping,

each one is snow-flake snapping,

lapping up the snow— Snow Happy!

We're packing snow and smacking,

we're dodging and we're whacking.

Snowballs fly and we're—
Snow Happy!

We're shoveling out the sidewalks,
making brand-new wide walks.
Gramp and Grammy look–

Snow
Happy!

Our snowman's tippy dumpy,
but none of us are grumpy.
We fix him up 'til he's—

Snow Happy!

We're trying to build an igloo,
an icy gleaming *bigloo*!

We dig, and pile, and pack—

Snow Happy!

In drifts where we were lying,

snow angels now are flying.

They stare up at the sky—

Snow Happy!

We're tired, cold, and soaking,
but we're laughing, shouting, joking,
tramping back indoors—

Snow Happy!

Drinking nice hot cocoa,
we watch the sparkling snow blow.
Winter makes us all—

So Happy!